Meghan Rose
IS Tickled Pinkish Orange

written by
Lori Z. Scott

illustrated by
Stacy Curtis

Standard®
PUBLISHING
Cincinnati, Ohio

Published by Standard Publishing, Cincinnati, Ohio
www.standardpub.com

Printed in: USA
Project editor: Diane Stortz

ISBN 978-0-7847-2933-5

Library of Congress Cataloging-in-Publication Data

Scott, Lori Z., 1965-
  Meghan Rose is tickled pinkish orange / written by Lori Z.
Scott ; illustrated by Stacy Curtis.
      p. cm.
  Summary: When Meghan Rose becomes the only girl on
her friend Ryan's soccer team, she experiences a range of
emotions and turns to God for help as she tries to learn the
game and be accepted as an equal.
  ISBN 978-0-7847-2933-5
  [1. Soccer--Fiction. 2. Christian life--Fiction. 3. Emotions-
-Fiction. 4. Sex role--Fiction. 5. Color--Fiction.] I. Curtis,
Stacy, ill. II. Title.
  PZ7.S42675Md 2011
  [Fic]--dc22
                                        2010040177

17 16 15 14 13 12 11   9 8 7 6 5 4 3 2 1

Contents

HA!
HA-
HA!
HA-
HA-
HA!
QUACK-
QUACK-
QUACK-
QUACK-
QUACK-
QUACK-
QUACK-
QUACK!

1

Green Field

On the sidelines of my school's soccer field, I lay on my back like a mummy (only not all wrapped up).

"The grass makes this the most comfy place on the playground to try out my idea," I told my friends. All of us lay in a jagged line, head to tummy, like a lightning bolt.

"I feel silly," Lynette said. She straightened her big hair bow. "What are we doing?"

"An experiment," I said. "I call it Exactly How Bouncy Are Stomachs? Kayla's Kangaroozie shoozies gave me the idea. The first person says *HA*. That should make the head lying on that tummy bounce once. The next person—that's you, Lynette—says *HA* twice, making the next head bounce twice."

"And I say *HA* three times," Ryan said.

"Kayla says *HA* four times," said Adam, and I—"

Lynette interrupted. "I get it! Let's start before I change my mind."

"Wait!" Kayla said. "I want to say *QUACK* instead."

"Fine," I said. I took a big breath. "*HA!*" I shouted. I felt Lynette's head bounce.

"*HA-HA!*" Lynette said.

"*HA-HA-HA!*" Ryan said.

I imagined Kayla's blond piggy tails flopping along with each *HA*. I stifled a giggle . . . and Lynette's head bounced another time. She huffed and fixed her hair bow again.

"Whee!" Kayla said. "My turn!" And then Kayla either lost count or lost control of her *QUACKS*. Or both. Because she didn't stop. "*QUACK-QUACK-QUACK-QUACK-QUACK-QUACK . . .*"

Adam's head bounced like a ping-pong ball in a blender. Which made me laugh. And before you could say pickle juice, everyone exploded with *HA-HA*s and *HEE-HEE*s and *HO-HO*s and *QUACK*s.

Heads went bouncy-wouncy, bouncy-wouncy, bouncy-wouncy on each mummy tummy, mummy tummy, mummy tummy, mummy tummy.

"S-s-stop!" Adam yelled. "L-l-l-let m-m-me off this c-c-crazy thing!"

Poor guy. Even his voice sounded bouncy-wouncy.

Still, we laughed and laughed and laughed. We laughed until my face hurt. We laughed until my sides ached. We laughed until tears rolled down my cheeks. We laughed until, with a happy sigh, I sat up.

Lynette rolled off. "Ouch," she said, rubbing her neck. "I've heard of being tickled pink, but I've never heard of being laughed black-and-blue."

"What do you mean?" Kayla said. "I'm not black or blue or pink."

"It's a joke," Lynette said. "Black-and blue means you feel bruised. Which, right now, I do. That's the opposite of being tickled pink, which means you feel exceptionally blissful."

I saw the puzzled look on Kayla's face. "*Exceptionally blissful* means really, really, really happy," I whispered.

"Then why not just say *really, really, really happy*?" Kayla whispered back.

"OK." I jumped to my feet. "I'M REALLY, REALLY, REALLY HAPPY! AND NOTHING IN THE WORLD CAN CHANGE THAT!"

Just then, WUMP, a soccer ball bounced our way. Before it hit anyone, I stopped it with my foot.

Looking up, I saw a boy running toward us. Drops of sweat oozed down his face, making his mop of yellow hair stick flat against his skin.

"Throw me the ball!" he yelled.

Instead, I took three steps and kicked

the ball as far as I could. It sailed over the boy's head, hit the middle of the green field, and bounced over three more boys before someone chased it down.

The mop-of-yellow-hair boy frowned at me and then sprinted back to the game.

"Wowie," Ryan said. "That was one powerful kick. How did you learn to kick like that?"

I shrugged. "My dad. Sometimes we kick my Purr-Purr Pretty Kitty ball in the backyard."

"A lot of boys on my soccer team can't kick that far," Ryan said. "Maybe you should join the team. Gabe got hurt last week, so we're short a player."

"You'd want a girl on your team?"

"Sure," Ryan said. "Some of the teams have boys and girls. And if you can kick like that, I want you on my team."

"But I've never played *real* soccer before."

"Then you're a natural!" Ryan said.

"Meghan's a boat?" Kayla said.

"No. You're thinking of *nautical*," Lynette said. "Being a *natural* means you are good at something without even trying!"

"So Meghan's good at being a boat?"

Lynette sighed. "Naturally."

Ryan ignored them. "Come on, Meghan! My dad's the coach. And I'll teach you everything you need to know."

"I'll do it!" I said. "If my parents say yes."

Then *TWEEEEEET*, the whistle blew, ending recess. I didn't even have time to wonder what I was getting myself into.

2

Red-Faced

"Team practice starts in twenty minutes," Ryan's dad—Coach Baker—said. "For now, we've got the whole field to ourselves so I can see how well Meghan plays before the others arrive. How do Ryan's old shin guards feel?"

"Like stiff tubes," I said.

Coach Baker laughed. I hoped that was a good thing. I wanted to WOW him. And not just because he was Ryan's dad or because

I wanted to tear around the field with my good friend. I had another fun reason to play soccer—laundry!

Usually, grass-stained, muddy, sweaty clothes get a sour-pickle look from my mom. But if I played on a team, my clothes could get grass-stained and muddy and sweaty . . . and I wouldn't get scolded for it!

Tap, tap, tap, *WUMP*. Tap, tap, tap, *WUMP*. Tap, tap, tap, *WUMP*. Ryan and I passed a soccer ball back and forth.

"Nice job, Meghan," Coach Baker finally said. "Are you sure you've never played before?"

"Just with my dad."

Coach Baker smiled. "You're good enough to play in our league and you're Ryan's friend. It will take some of the boys a little time to get used to the idea of playing with a girl . . . but . . . welcome to the team!"

"Yay!" I screamed. I ran around the field waving my hands. "Yay! Yay! Yay! It's time to do the happy dance!"

"No!" Ryan yelled. He looked over his shoulder. "Meghan! Not now!"

But I had too much happy in me to stop. I went wiggle, wiggle up! Wiggle, wiggle down! Wiggle, spin, wiggle, spin, wiggle to the ground—

"What are you doing?" I heard a not-glad-to-see-you-sounding voice say. "And why are you here, anyway?"

That wasn't Coach Baker's voice. Or Ryan's voice.

Biting my lip, I glanced up. That wasn't Coach Baker's or Ryan's face looking down at me, either.

It was the mop-of-yellow-hair boy from the playground. In his arms he held the same soccer ball I had kicked over his head. And here I was, his new teammate, lying on the ground, looking more like a natural worm than a natural soccer player.

My heart went *BUMP-bump*. I turned red-faced . . . which is another way of saying *gulp*. All my happy left in a snappy. Swallowing hard, I stood up.

Coach Baker put a hand on my shoulder. "Zayne, this is Meghan Thompson. She's taking Gabe's place on our team."

"She's a *girl*," Zayne said. He made *girl* sound like a bad word.

"She's a soccer player," Coach Baker said. "She's got decent skills, but she doesn't know all the rules yet. We can help her out. Right?"

Zayne frowned, but he nodded. Then when Coach Baker turned around to greet some other players, Zayne glared at Ryan. "Was *she* your idea?"

"Yes," Ryan said. "You can thank me later."

I put my hands on my hips. "My name isn't *she*. It's Meghan."

"Don't let her touch me," Zayne said to Ryan. "*She* has germs."

"Stop calling me she!" I said.

Zayne gave Ryan a look. "What did *she* just say?"

"She said—oops!—I mean Meghan said . . . uh—"

Another boy joined us. "Hi, Jarrett," Ryan said.

"Hi. Who's Meghan?"

"*She* is," Zayne said. "*She* is Gabe's

replacement. And *she* has germs."

"Fine," I snapped. "Get ready for germs then. Because I'm going to show you what *she* can do."

Then I snatched the ball out of his hands and drop-kicked it across the field.

"Awesome!" Jarrett said.

"Hey! That was my ball!" Zayne yelled. Then he tripped over his shoelaces running after it. And turn as red-faced as I had.

"Don't worry about Zayne," Ryan said. "Once he sees how well you play, he'll forget you're a girl."

I folded my arms across my chest. "Are you saying girls can't play soccer as well as boys?"

"No!" said Ryan.

Then Coach Baker blew his whistle. We circled up and he introduced everyone: Ryan (of course!), Zayne, Jarrett, Caleb, Steve, Bryson, R. J., Nate, and me.

When we warmed up, I outran everyone but Ryan. Then I breezed through ball drills. I felt happy again . . . until we scrimmaged.

Scrimmaging means to split the players into two teams. The teams play each other like it's a real game. And scrimmages get rough.

When I outran people, they tripped me. If I got close to the goal, someone elbowed me. And no one but Ryan or Jarrett passed me the ball.

Plus, in a voice loud enough to be heard by me but not Coach Baker, Zayne kept saying things like, "*She* plays like a girl." And "*She* looks tired." And "*She* isn't as good as Gabe."

So by the time we finished, I didn't have

a single happy bone in my body.

"Nice practice," Ryan said when we got in his car to go home.

"Except Zayne hates me."

"Don't let Zayne bother you," Ryan said.

But I did.

3

Feeling Blue

The next day at school, I didn't have my usual kangaroo bounciness.

My first-grade teacher, Mrs. Arnold, noticed. She felt my forehead twice during science.

"I'm fine," I said. "I just lost all my happy."

"So you're feeling blue?" she said.

"If blue means sad, then yes," I said.

My body still felt droopy-droop when Ryan and I got on the bus to go home.

"Zayne?" Ryan asked.

I nodded.

Ryan pulled out a copy of *Super Cat*, his favorite comic book. "You need Super Cat to save the day!"

I perked up. "Let's pretend he does!" I said. "I know how to start. First Clawdia, the girl cat who always needs saving, cries, 'Help! The evil chicken, Zayne, used his fowl feather weapon to wipe out laughter.'"

Ryan grinned. "Then Zayne forces Clawdia to watch television sitcom reruns. The laugh tracks are gone, so the bad jokes are even worse!"

"Poor Clawdia," I said.

"Plus Zayne threw eggs on the heads of all the cartoonists in the city," Ryan said. "Now they can't crack a smile. None of them can draw because *the yokes on them*."

"And let's pretend Zayne raided the library and punched out all the punch lines in the joke books," I said. "Now they don't make sense! Why did the chicken cross the road? Peanut butter! How many dogs does it take to change a light bulb? Peanut butter! Knock, knock. Who's there? Peanut butter!"

"Is there no hope?" Ryan said.

"Um . . . I don't know. Is there?"

"Of course!" Ryan said. "Because Super Cat knows something is wrong in Cat City. He has watched the laughless shows. He has read the newspapers with no comics. He has seen the joke books with no jokes."

"So what does he do?" I asked.

Ryan said, "Super Cat checks his main weapons: armpit odor, a spray bottle of dirty-sock smell, and hairball pellets with a slingshot. Now he's ready to battle Zayne. To the Cat Mobile!"

"He needs to save Clawdia first," I said.

"OK. First, he finds Clawdia. It's easy because there's a big arrow sign that says, 'Clawdia Is Here.'"

"But Clawdia is stuck in a squishy couch that has drinks, snacks, and a potty," I said. "So she has no reason to escape."

"Except she can't stand to watch another rerun," Ryan said. "So Super Cat asks, 'Where is the remote control?' And Clawdia says, 'Right over there. But the batteries are dead.'"

I said, "Then Super Cat growls, 'I'll have to do this the hard way.' And carefully he extends his claws to full scratch mode."

"Oh no!" Ryan gasped with a la-de-da voice. "You've got a hangnail!"

"Very funny," I said. "Then, with a heroic effort, Super Cat presses the off button on the TV."

"Now they can save the newspaper cartoonists," Ryan said.

"And fix the joke books," I said.

Ryan paused. "Well, I actually think 'Peanut butter' is a pretty funny line. So I don't see a problem there."

"Fine," I said. "So the two cats hightail it out the door toward the newsroom. They take the stairs since neither one can reach the elevator buttons. They go at least one hundred meows per hour."

Ryan waved a finger in the air. "But as

WHERE IS
THE REMOTE
CONTROL?

they burst out of the stairwell, Zayne is waiting for them. Super Cat grabs his spray bottle. Zayne swats it away. Super Cat loads a hairball pellet. The slingshot backfires!"

"Super Cat groans, 'We surrender,'" I said. "And he starts to raise his arms—"

"But then," Ryan interrupted, "Zayne stops him. 'I know all about your terrible armpit odor,' he says. 'Keep your paws down.'"

I laughed. "Good one! Now Zayne slowly circles Clawdia and Super Cat, poking them with a turkey feather."

Ryan lowered his voice. "And Zayne says, 'You have fallen into my cluck-cluck-clutches once again.'"

"But Super Cat says, 'We'll stop you!'"

"Zayne just spits on the floor, which is rather hard for a chicken to do," Ryan said. "Zayne cackles, 'Don't make me laugh.'"

I snapped my fingers. "Suddenly, Super Cat knows that's EXACTLY what he must do! He blurts out, 'Knock, knock.' Zayne cannot resist asking, 'Who's there?' Then Super Cat says, 'Sarah.'"

"Sarah who?" asked Ryan.

"Sarah reason you're not laughing?" I said.

"Ha-ha," Ryan said. "My turn. Before Zayne can stop him, Super Cat says again, 'Knock, knock.' Zayne twists in agony, but cannot stop from saying—"

"Who's there?"

"Luke."

"Luke who?"

"Luke out, here comes another knock-knock joke."

"Boo!" I said. "Zayne shrieks and stumbles across the room."

"And Super Cat says, 'Knock, knock,'" said Ryan.

"Who's there?"

"Goliath."

"Goliath who?"

"Goliath down, you looketh tired. Knock, knock."

I stopped Ryan before he could get too carried away. "At that last 'Knock, knock,' Zayne topples over SPLAT on the floor. Super Cat smiles and says, 'Imagine that! I just knock-knocked him out!'"

"Once again, joy is restored to Cat City. The end," Ryan said as we pulled up to his bus stop. "Feel better?"

"Yes," I said, with a big smile. "My happy is all back!"

And I knew what to do the next time Zayne bugged me. I'd crack a few jokes and save the day with laughter.

Of course, Super Cat never played soccer with Zayne.

4
Feeling Yellow

"I'm playing soccer at recess today," I told Lynette and Kayla the next morning.

Lynette checked off her name on the lunch chart and handed the marker to Kayla. "Why? We almost always jump rope."

"My first real soccer game is in three days," I said. "Playing soccer during recess might help me get ready for it. Besides, I'm hoping I can get a boy named Zayne to laugh at my jokes and say I'm a great teammate.

Then I'll live happily ever after."

"Who's Zayne?" Kayla asked.

"A boy on my soccer team," I said.

"And he doesn't laugh at your jokes?"

"I actually haven't told him any jokes yet," I said.

"Then don't expect him to laugh."

I sighed. "It's just for a few days until I learn everything Ryan knows about soccer."

"Good!" Kayla said. "But that should only take five minutes."

"You can play too," I said.

"No thanks," Lynette said. "We'll watch. Right, Kayla?"

"Yay!" Kayla said. "I've never seen a boat play soccer before."

"She's still confused about the *natural* thing," Lynette whispered.

"Naturally," I whispered back.

"We'll cheer for you!" Kayla said. "Lynette can yell, 'Go, Meghan, go!' And I'll yell, 'Quack, quacky, quack!' That's duck talk for 'Go, Meghan, go!'"

Then Kayla flapped her arms and did a wacky duck walk.

My heart went *BUMP-bump*. What would Zayne do if Kayla started wacky-quacking from the sidelines?

"Thanks, but no thanks!" I said quickly.

"But what if you get on the field and start feeling yellow?" Lynette said. "We could encourage you!"

"I don't feel yellow."

"Feel yellow?" Kayla said. "Do you mean touching bananas and lemons . . . and DUCKS? I want to feel yellow!"

Lynette rolled her eyes. "No, you don't.

Feeling yellow means you're scared. My dad always tells me not to feel yellow before dance recitals."

"Oh," Kayla said with a frown. "Well, that's no fun."

All morning I watched the clock. And prayed that Zayne would like my jokes and like my kicks and like me. Then I'd get all my happy back.

But as lunchtime got closer, my tummy started doing flips.

If I hadn't known better, I'd have said I felt a little bit . . . GULP . . . yellow. Or maybe a *lot* yellow. Or . . .

"Kayla," I said as we lined up for lunch, "I think I'd rather jump rope with you at recess after all."

"Don't be silly," Kayla said. "Boats don't jump rope."

"Boats don't play soccer, either," I snapped.

"Oh yeah?" Kayla said. "Then why do soccer teams have captains?"

How could I argue with that? So Ryan and I went straight to the soccer field at recess.

"Meghan!" Jarrett said when he saw me. "Are you playing?"

I nodded.

"Excellent!" Jarrett said, giving me a high five. That put some bounce in my step.

Zayne frowned at me. "*She* can't play."

"Really?" I said. Time to see if I could make Zayne laugh. "Well, all I have to say is . . . Knock, knock."

Zayne looked surprised. But he said, "Who's there?"

"Yukon."

29

"Yukon who?"

"Yukon't stop me!" I said. I gave Zayne my friendliest smile.

Ryan, Jarrett, and some others laughed. Zayne didn't.

"Knock, knock," I said again.

It seemed like everyone answered this time. "Who's there?"

"Our wee iguana."

"Our wee iguana who?"

"Our wee iguana play, or what?" I said.

More laughter. Even Zayne flashed a quick smile, but then he glanced away.

"OK," Zayne said. "*She* can play." He looked at Ryan. "But not on my team."

So we played. Lynette and Kayla watched. Luckily, they didn't cheer. Except the one time I stole the ball from Zayne and Kayla let out a big QUACK! before Lynette shushed her.

By the end of recess, Zayne was calling me by my real name. Even so, he seemed to play harder and rougher whenever I was near.

I think I showed Zayne I was good enough to help his soccer team. But even my clever jokes didn't seem to make him like me any better. And THAT was an unhappy thought.

5

Black Mood

When recess ended, Lynette hugged me. "I didn't know you could play so well."

I shrugged. "Neither did I. But it doesn't matter."

"It sounds like you're in a black mood," she said.

"Stop using all those colorful words," I complained. "I don't know what you mean."

Lynette gave me an I-know-something-you-don't smile. (I do not hold that against her because she actually does know a lot of things I don't.) "A black mark means you fail at something. A black mood means there is not even one ounce of happy in your whole body."

I didn't know what an ounce was, but since it sounded like the word *bounce*, it seemed about right. Zayne had taken all my bounce away.

On the bus ride home, I slouched in my seat.

"Are you ready for soccer practice tonight?" Ryan asked.

"No," I said. "I'm in a black mood. That means there is not even one bounce of happy in my whole body."

Ryan grinned. "I bet I can change that." He pulled a small package out of his backpack and tossed it to me.

"Jelly beans?"

"Leftover from my lunch," Ryan said.

"Since when do you leave candy uneaten?"

"Since Easter," Ryan said.

I rolled my eyes. "And you think jelly beans will solve my problem? Thanks, but no thanks. I'm not hungry." I tossed them back to him.

Ryan pushed them back into my hand. "Keep them. You'll thank me later."

"I already thanked you. Just now. And then no-thanked you too."

"Ha! Humor! That's what you need—a good joke," Ryan said. "What do you get when you cross a tree with a tiger?"

I turned away. "I'm in a black mood, remember. I'm not in the mood for jokes."

"A cat that barks!" Ryan answered, completely ignoring me. Then he rattled off more jokes, one after the other, *BAM*, *BAM*, *BAM*, like popcorn. "What do you call a jumpy zebra? A hyper striper. What do you get when you cross a parrot with a sloth? An animal that talks r-e-a-l-l-y slow. What do you call a squished hippo? A hippopota-MUSH!"

"Ryan!" I snapped. "Enough with the animal jokes! How can you laugh at a time like this?"

The grin fell off Ryan's face like ice cream off a cone. "I guess I can't."

Now we were both in a black mood.

Black like the black jelly beans mixed in with the colored ones in the package Ryan gave me.

I stuffed the jelly beans down in my

backpack. Too bad I couldn't do that with my black mood.

Dear God, I prayed, *I don't need a short laugh from another lame joke. I need a happy that lasts a little longer than that.*

6

Orange You Glad?

"Ryan will be here soon to pick you up for soccer practice," Mom said. She handed me my shin guards and socks. "You'll need to fill your water bottle, use the bathroom, put on your shoes, eat a snack, and put your hair in a ponytail. Hurry up!"

For some reason, that made me move even slower.

With a sigh, Mom grabbed my brush and started to work on my hair.

"You seem distracted," she said.

"I'm in a black mood."

"Because of soccer?"

"Kind of," I said.

"But you still want to play?" Mom asked.

"Yes."

"Are you OK with playing on a boys' team?"

"Ryan's one of my best friends," I said.

"But?"

I frowned. "Not everyone on the team is my friend."

"Don't worry," Mom said, twisting the ponytail holder around my hair. "The boys will get used to you. In the meantime, don't let them get you down."

"I tried telling jokes," I said. "But with jokes, you laugh once and it's over. I want a

happy that lasts."

Mom thought for a minute. "I'm not sure happy means that everyone always likes you and nothing bad ever happens. Besides, if you never know what it's like to be sad, how will you know when you're happy?"

"Oh," I said in a small voice.

"The Bible says there is a time for everything," Mom continued. "There are times to cry and times to laugh. Times to be sad and times to dance." Then she started singing and dancing the cha-cha around my room.

She's that kind of mother.

And . . . I hopped up and joined in.

I'm that kind of kid.

We yowled and danced and sang until I felt dizzy with laughter.

Finally we stopped to catch our breath.

"Does that mean I can't do anything about the weird up-down, smile-frown roller-coaster ride I've been on?" I asked.

Mom tilted her head. "Not necessarily. The Bible also says, 'Always be full of joy in the Lord.' *Always* means at all times, no matter what."

"So even though there's a time to cry, I can still choose to be happy?" I asked.

Mom nodded. "I think so."

I made a huffy sound. "But that's what I don't get! How can I *choose* to be happy when I don't *feel* happy?"

"Perhaps you can start by remembering all the things you have to be happy about in the first place," Mom said. "And then keep on, keep on, *keep on* remembering them. Can you do that?"

"I'll try," I said.

41

"Good. Now, you haven't eaten a snack. What would you like?"

I remembered Ryan's jelly beans. "I've got something in my backpack."

"OK," Mom said. She checked her watch. "Five minutes. I'll fill up your water bottle."

I tore open the package and sorted the jelly beans by color. I quick-picked out my favorites—yellow, purple, and green—and popped them in my mouth. Then I laid out the colors that were left.

One black, four reds, one white, and three orange.

Black like a bad mood. Or a black mark. Lynette said a black mark meant failure. And I had failed at making friends with Zayne.

Red, the color of Christmas! Yay! At Christmas we celebrate Jesus' birthday. But red is also the color of blood.

I touched the black jelly bean and then a red one. I had a lot of black marks in my life, but Jesus said, "I'll erase all your black marks for you."

I knew that because Dad had read to me in the Bible about how Jesus bled and died and lived again. Jesus covered my black marks with his own red blood. He covered the black marks for everyone.

Even Zayne, I thought as I threw the black jelly bean in the trash and popped the red jelly beans in my mouth. *Wowie*.

The white jelly bean reminded me of Mrs. Arnold's whiteboard, without a single black mark on it.

I ate the white jelly bean. Then I put all three orange ones in my mouth. They reminded me of Ryan's lame knock-knock jokes—"Orange you glad I didn't say banana again?"

It made me think . . . orange you glad for friends? Orange you glad for food? Orange you glad you can pray and talk to God?

BLAM! Something clicked in my mind. The jelly beans told a story! With his red blood, Jesus erased my black marks and left my heart cleaner than Mrs. Arnold's whiteboard. Orange you glad?

And since that was true . . . maybe happy didn't depend on what was going on around me. Maybe happy depended more on what was going on *inside* me. And inside me I could always hold on to the biggest happy thought ever: God loves me, black marks and all!

No one could take that kind of happy away from me. And . . . I could share it!

I HAD to do the happy dance. Wiggle, wiggle up! Wiggle, wiggle down! Wiggle, spin, wiggle, and—

"Meghan!" Mom yelled. "Time to go!"

I grabbed the jelly bean bag to throw it away and felt a lump inside. Hey! There was one perfectly pink jelly bean left.

I popped it in my mouth and ran down the stairs feeling tickled pinkish orange-you-glad!

7

Cha-Cha

Tap, tap, tap, *WUMP*. Tap, tap, tap, *WUMP*. Ryan and I were passing the ball together when Zayne arrived for practice.

"Hi, Zayne," Ryan said. "Do you want to pass with us?"

Zayne made a face. "I would. But *she*'s getting germs all over the ball."

That mean comment made those old black-mood feelings start to trickle into my mind. So I zippy-quick remembered my big happy thought: God loves me. God loves Zayne too. I took a big breath and smiled.

"It's OK, Zayne," I said. "You can pass with Ryan. Jarrett's here now, so I'll pass with him."

Zayne's face looked like someone had just slapped him. "Uh . . . OK . . . thanks."

"No problem," I said, giving Jarrett a high five.

At least Zayne said thanks. That was a start.

Later, we ran laps to warm up. Zayne finished right behind me.

"Good run," I told him.

He just glared at me, breathing hard.

Coach Baker cuffed Zayne on the shoulder. "I've never seen you run so fast. Keep it up."

Next, we played a game like tag. First

everyone dribbles onto the field. Then you have to protect your own ball while trying to kick all the other balls out of bounds. If your ball gets kicked out of bounds, you're out. The last person left on the field wins.

Zayne went after me and after me and after me. He said a few mean things too, but I didn't answer him. I just smiled and kept moving.

That seemed to annoy Zayne even more. He focused so hard on getting me out, he missed Ryan coming up from behind him to kick his ball out of bounds.

From the look on Zayne's face, I could tell he wasn't used to losing. I could also tell by the look on Coach Baker's face that he didn't mind Zayne working harder than usual because of me.

Before we scrimmaged at the end of

practice, Coach Baker showed the team a new passing skill. Step left, step right. Left step over the ball. Right kick backwards and to the left.

"It's a sneak pass to confuse your defender," Coach Baker said. "It looks easy, but it will take practice to learn it well enough to use in a game."

So we practiced. Step left, step right, step, kick. Step left, step right, step, kick.

The sneak pass had its own beat. It reminded me of Mom's dance. Cha-cha, cha-cha, cha, CHA! Step-left, step-right, step, KICK!

"Coach!" I yelled. "I did it! And . . . it's like a DANCE!"

Coach Baker came over. The boys stopped and watched. I lined up two balls several feet apart. Then I started singing the cha-cha and doing the tricky footwork. "Cha-cha, cha-cha, cha, CHA! Cha-cha, cha-cha, cha, CHA!"

Two balls rolled across the field in a very sneaky way.

"You DID do it!" Coach Baker said. "Excellent!"

I grinned. "We should call it the sneaky-pass cha-cha."

Zayne yelled, "No!"

Coach Baker yelled, "PERFECT!"

"Dancing is a *girl* thing," Zayne grumped under his breath. He glanced my way, so I winked at him.

Ryan grabbed a ball. "Let me try it!" he said. He put on a goofy grin and waved his hands like a cheerleader. Then he did the steps and sang in a high squeaky voice, "Cha-cha, cha-cha, cha, CHA!"

The ball rolled across the field in a very sneaky way. It stopped in front of Jarrett.

Ryan's mouth opened so wide, you could have put a soccer ball in it. "It works!" he yelled. "It really works!"

Then everyone on the team—and even Zayne—scrambled zippy-quick for a ball and started doing the sneaky-pass cha-cha.

When we scrimmaged, we all tried to use our new move. And we all ended up losing the ball when we tried it too. Coach Baker was right. We would need more practice.

Zayne played hard and rough, but he didn't say anything mean.

"So . . . are you ready for the game tomorrow?" I asked him when practice ended.

"Sure," he said.

"Are you excited?"

"I guess."

"What's your jersey number?"

"8."

"You're a really good player," I said. "It makes me feel sorry for the other team."

Zayne stared at me. "Why are you being so nice?"

I shrugged. "It makes me happy."

Then a car horn honked.

"Your ride is here," I said. "Bye."

Shaking his head, Zayne turned to leave. "*Girls!*" he muttered.

8

The Game

"Mom, please don't tie a ribbon around my ponytail," I said, pushing her hand away. "Soccer is not a fashion show!"

"But it matches your jersey perfectly!" Mom said.

"So does the living room sofa, but I'm not wearing the sofa on my head."

"I only want you to look nice for your first soccer game." She straightened my shirt and looked at my feet. "Did you double knot your shoelaces?"

"Yes, Mom," I said. "And I have my water bottle. I'm wearing my shin guards. I put on sunscreen and bug spray."

"OK," Mom said. "Ryan is here to pick you up. Dad and I will be there when the game starts. Good luck!"

As we pulled into the soccer fields, my

hands started getting sweaty. Coach Baker made us warm up, and soon my tummy flips went away. Because another team in red jerseys was already warming up . . . and they looked T-A-L-L.

I grabbed Ryan's arm. "Tell me those aren't first graders."

"Those aren't first graders," Ryan said. Then he leaned closer and said, "They actually ARE first graders, but you asked me not to tell you that."

"Ryan!" I yelled.

He laughed. "We played this team in the fall. They beat us."

"Don't worry," Coach Baker said. "We've got Meghan this time. Besides, I always say, 'The bigger they are, the harder they fall.'"

"That's funny," I said. "I always say,

'The bigger they are, the faster you'd better clear out!'"

I didn't have any more time to worry about the other team. Coach Baker made us warm up, and soon my tummy flips went away. My hands were still sweaty, but so were my face and neck and arms.

The officials lined up each team and checked shin guards and shoes. Then captains — in our case, Ryan — were called to choose sides. The rest of our team huddled up to talk strategy. "Talk strategy" means the coach reminds you, "Everyone figure out how to kick the ball into the goal and don't trip on your shoelaces."

I felt kangaroo bouncy and ready for action . . . until I heard the other team laughing. I looked over and saw seven sets of eyes looking back at me.

Then in a loud voice, someone said, "They have a *girl* on their team."

And someone else replied, "They're all *girls*."

My cheeks flushed hot. Zayne looked my way and slammed his ball into the ground. I felt my happy excitement begin to drain away.

But I remembered what I learned from my jelly beans. I squeezed my eyes shut and prayed, *Thank you, God, for everything I have to be happy about. Like Mom. Dad. My friends. SHIN GUARDS! And the fact that I can run fast if I need to. AMEN!*

Since I was the newest player on our team, I didn't start on the field. I knew my time would come, though. Coach Baker used a stopwatch to make sure everyone played an equal amount.

WOWIE. I thought practice scrimmages were rough. I had no idea how hard players run and kick and push in a real game! And did I mention the other team was T-A-L-L? Not only that, it didn't take long for them to S-C-O-R-E.

Plus, by the way Ryan frowned, I could tell the red team was making comments about me.

Then Coach Baker put his hand on my shoulder. "I need some speed and sneak out there, Meghan. Can you give me that?"

I nodded.

"Good," he said. "Because you're my secret weapon."

"I am?"

"The other team won't expect you to score. They're thinking, *She's a girl. Don't worry about her.* You pour on the steam, zip past them, and kick it in."

I gave him a sly smile. "I like that plan."

"SUB, REF!" Coach Baker yelled.

9

True Colors

BUMP-bump. *BUMP-bump.* *BUMP-bump.* My heart pounded like a rainstorm. I chased the ball wherever it went. And got elbowed and pushed and kicked.

"UH!" I grunted, booting the ball. It sailed out of bounds.

"Control the ball, Meghan!" Coach Baker yelled. "Dribble it up the field."

The red team threw the ball in. I chased it down but kicked it out of bounds again.

"Is that all girls can do?" a red player shouted. "Kick it out of bounds?"

"Hey, knock it off!" Ryan shouted back.

"Why? Is she your *girlfriend*?" the boy sneered.

Before Ryan could answer, the ball was in play again.

When I subbed out, Coach Baker didn't seem to notice my hard breathing.

"Nice hustle, Meghan," he said. "But you can't score from the middle of the field. Drive to the goal and score from there. You've got the speed. Where's your sneak?"

When I went in again, Zayne had the ball. I knew he wouldn't pass it to me, so I watched the other players instead.

Everyone was tangled together like hairballs. All except me and the red team's best player, number 13. He stood alone, wide open, like he was waiting for something . . .

Which meant if Zayne lost the ball, the red team would probably pass it to him!

Zoom! I took off across the field. Sure enough, a red player stole the ball from Zayne and kicked it toward number 13. But—*SNEAK ATTACK*—I leaped in front of him and stole the ball back.

Then I poured on my speed!

Just like Coach Baker predicted, the other team didn't expect a *girl* to score.

But I did.

At halftime, we were down 3–1.

"Get a drink," Coach Baker ordered.

Grabbing my water bottle, I plopped down on the bench. Ryan plopped down next to me.

"Yuck," I said. "You're covered in grass stains and sweat."

He shrugged. "Double yuck. So are you. Plus you bruised your knee."

I touched my knee. Ouch. "You're right. I didn't notice," I said. "It doesn't matter. I can't wait to get back on the field. I know we can BEAT them!"

Ryan frowned.

I grinned. Sure, we were losing and the red players said mean things, but I was doing my best, and I felt—happy!

Coach Baker got our attention. "They might be bigger than us, but they're slower," he said. "We need to move the ball around more. Spread out, find someone open, and pass the ball."

We took the field again.

Coach Baker started me this time. His kickoff plan was for Ryan to sprint down the field. Then Zayne would tap the ball to me. Then I'd give it a huge kick to Ryan for the score.

It worked. Tap, BOOM, dribble-dribble, BOOT! Thirty seconds later, Ryan scored.

My team whooped and hollered.

The other coach threw his hat on the ground. And said some interesting words about being beaten by a girl. After that, the red team seemed to play pushier and angrier. Especially number 13.

But we were still down 3–2. Jarrett stole the ball and passed it to me. I dribbled past a defender, straight toward the goal.

"Come on!" number 13 screamed. "Don't let a germy *girl* beat you!"

"Leave her alone!" another voice yelled. "She might be a germy girl, but she's OUR germy girl!"

That sounded like . . . Zayne?!

Then WHAM! I went down hard on the
ground. The red defender couldn't catch up,

so he had decided to slide tackle me. Which
isn't allowed in our league.

And also hurts.

The whistle blew to stop play. Coach Baker ran over to check on me. The rest of the team crowded around too.

"I'm fine," I said, rubbing my leg. "How much time is left?"

"Less than a minute," Coach Baker said. "We have time to kick—"

Then BLAM! I remembered the Bible verse Mom shared with me.

"Coach!" I said, "There's a time to kick and there's a time to dance! How do you feel about the cha-cha?"

"Very sneaky," he said. "Can you do it?"

"I know she can," Zayne said. "After all, dancing is for *girls*."

We all laughed.

"Let's go!" the referee yelled.

"Let's dance!" I whispered to Zayne.

We spread out and took our places.

Jarrett kicked the ball to me and . . . cha-cha, cha-cha, cha, CHA! Defenders lunged right toward Ryan . . . and I sent the ball *left* toward Zayne.

Who—BOOM—scored!

The game ended in a 3–3 tie. Zayne was the big hero. And I was the happiest player on the field.

10

Tickled Pinkish Orange

I sat in a circle of kids on the playground. Lynette sat in the middle.

"What are we playing?" Lynette asked.

"It's a game called Don't Make Me Laugh," I said. "Your job is to try and make the rest of us laugh. You can make goofy faces, dance, sing . . . do whatever it takes—without tickling—to make us laugh. Whoever laughs first is IT next."

Lynette rolled her eyes. "And why are

70

we playing this?"

"Because it's fun, of course," I said. "Now everyone . . . blank faces!"

Lynette lay down on her back.

"You can start now," I said.

"I did start," Lynette said. "Can't you tell I'm acting in an exceptionally blissful and highly entertaining manner?"

"No," I said. "You're using big words and facing the sky."

"Oh bother," Lynette said. Sitting up, she scooted in front of Kayla. She leaned close. Kayla sat up straight.

Lynette leaned closer. Kayla's eyes got big.

Lynette leaned even closer. Kayla's eyes got even wider. She sat up even straighter. Plus I saw her nostrils quiver.

"Quack," Lynette said.

"BAH-ha-ha-ha-ha!" Kayla burst out. "HAHAHAHAHAHAHAHAHAHA!" She flopped over backwards, kicked the ground, and flapped her arms.

"You're it!" Lynette yelled, switching places with Kayla.

Gasping for breath, Kayla crawled into the circle. With a big sigh, she let go of her giggles. Then she sat still for a minute, looking around the circle.

We didn't budge.

We didn't budge.

We didn't budge.

Then . . .

"QUACK!" Kayla flopped over backwards again, kicked the ground, and flapped her arms.

She looked so silly, everyone laughed along with her.

"HAHAHAHAHAHAHAHAHAHA!"

"You're ALL it!" Kayla said.

"*Whee!*" I said. "Let's do the happy dance!"

And we did. Wiggle, wiggle up! Wiggle, wiggle down! Wiggle, spin, wiggle, spin, wiggle to the ground. Wiggle, wiggle high! Wiggle, wiggle low! Wiggle, spin, wiggle, spin, everywhere you go!

We started the game over with someone new in the middle. And you'll never guess who it was.

Zayne.

That's right. Zayne.

He had a big smile on his face and a pack of jelly beans in his pocket.

I know . . . because I'm the one who gave them both to him.

I think I'm getting the hang of happy. It

has a lot to do with showing your true colors, especially when your true colors show that you love God and God loves you.

That's why at lunch I'd offered Zayne a package of jelly beans. As it turns out, Zayne really likes jelly beans (even the black ones). And then Ryan and I asked him if he wanted to play Don't Make Me Laugh with us and told him how it works.

At first he frowned. Then he shrugged and said, "Sure, I'll play. But only if I get to sit next to Meghan."

Ryan snickered.

Zayne said, "What?" and smacked him on the shoulder. But I could tell it was a friendly kind of smack.

Jarrett and Bryson and Steve and a bunch of other soccer players joined us too. But with a game like Don't Make Me Laugh, the more people you have, the more fun it is to play.

So Zayne sat in the middle of the circle, looking at a bunch of blank faces.

He turned to Jarrett and stuck out his tongue.

Jarrett didn't budge.

Zayne made a silly face.

Jarrett didn't budge.

Zayne did a goofy robot dance.

Jarrett didn't budge.

Zayne got right up in Jarrett's face and said, "Quack."

And KAYLA, sitting on the complete opposite side of the circle, flopped over backwards, kicked the ground, and flapped her arms, laughing. "BAH-ha-ha-ha-ha!"

That girl has some serious duck issues.

Even so, that recess ended up being one

of the giggliest recesses ever.

I was the grandest giggler of all. Because I knew that no matter what happens, if I keep remembering that God loves me, I'll always be happy deep down where it counts. Plus maybe I'll be a nicer and kinder person.

Let me end by saying two things.

First, what do you know, Ryan was right! I *did* end up thanking him later for the jelly beans. And Zayne thanked him later too, for asking me to join the team.

Second, if Zayne or anyone else tries to upset me again, I know what my answer will be.

Peanut butter.

OK, maybe not. (But it made you feel all tickled pinkish orange, didn't it?)

Chatter Matters

1. Another word for *happy* is *joy*. What does the Bible say about joy? Read Habakkuk 3:18–19, Acts 2:28, Romans 15:13, 1 Thessalonians 5:15–17, and 1 Peter 1:7–9. (Read one verse a day if you'd like.) Then tell in your own words what you think these verses mean. Can you give an example of when you have felt or seen this kind of joy? Do you have this kind of joy? If not, pray about it.

2. Think about a happy moment in your life. Tell what you remember about it.

3. Think about a time you cheered someone up. What did you do? Why do you think it worked? How did it make you feel?

4. Orange-you-glad about a lot of things? List ten things that make you happy.

5. What's the funniest joke you can think of?

Blam! – Great Activity Ideas

1. Get some friends together and play the Don't Make Me Laugh game from the last chapter of the book.

2. Grab a handful of jelly beans. Sort them by color. Which color do you have the most of? The least? Can you remember which jelly beans Meghan used to figure out the secret of being happy? If so, can you retell what she learned? Don't forget to eat the jelly beans when you're done. Yum!

3. Meghan and her friends talk a lot about colors in this story. Here's a colorful project you can try. You'll need food coloring, liquid dish soap, skim milk at room temperature, and a shallow bowl.

Pour milk into the bowl. Around the edges of the bowl, put several drops of different colored food coloring. Then add several drops of liquid dish soap to the center of the bowl . . . and watch what happens.

4. Check out a joke book from the library. Get together with a friend and take turns telling each other jokes.

5. Write your own Super Cat adventure. Here is the start:

Super Cat wants to bake cookies. He has all the ingredients for the recipe except . . . "Where are those chocolate chips?" he asks.

He searches the pantry but is unable to find them. He does, however, locate a bottle of chocolate syrup.

"My cookies are saved!" he cries. "I'll use chocolate syrup instead of chocolate chips!"

Little does he know, but this is NOT a good baking trade. The cookies mutate. They turn out as hard as hockey pucks. Perhaps even harder. He decides to taste one anyway, but it's so heavy, he drops it first. The cookie shatters the tile on his kitchen floor.

However, our hero has no time to worry about his ruined cookies or ruined floor, for just at that moment, Zayne bursts into the room. He drags Clawdia along with him. Zayne knows it's always best to bring a prisoner with you when you break into a superhero's house.

Zayne pauses. "I smell cookies," he snarls. "What kind?"

"They were supposed to be chocolate chip,"

Super Cat stutters. "But—"

"No buts," Zayne says, brandishing a turkey feather. "Hand them over, or the girl gets it."

Super Cat glances at the cookies. They might knock out a hippo if thrown hard enough.

"I'll just . . . toss them over," Super Cat says, reaching for the closest cookie.

Then Super Cat hesitates. The cookie might hit Clawdia. Should he take the risk?

Now you finish the story.

*For the Cooks: Jonene, Jeremy, Jarrett,
Jadrian, and Jereson—LZS*

For Rebekah—SC

Lori Z. Scott graduated from Wheaton
College eons ago. She is a second-grade teacher,
a wife, the mother of two busy teenagers, and a
writer. Lori has published over one hundred articles,
short stories, devotions, puzzles, and poems and has
contributed to over a dozen books.

In her spare time Lori loves doodling, reading the
Sunday comics, and making up lame jokes.

You can find out more about Lori and her books
at www.MeghanRoseSeries.com.

Stacy Curtis is a cartoonist, illustrator,
printmaker, and twin who's illustrated over twenty
children's books, including a *New York Times* best
seller. He and his wife, Jann, live in Oak Lawn,
Illinois, and happily share their home with their dog,
Derby.